The Submissive Sissy

A sissy maid and his mistress

Lady Alexa

Copyright © Lady Alexa 2016 & 2022

This novel is a work of fiction. Names, characters, businesses, places, events and incidents are either the products of the author's imagination or used in a fictitious manner. Any resemblance to actual persons, living or dead, or actual events is purely coincidental.

This erotic novel contains graphic scenes of a sexual nature including gender transformation, female domination, humiliation and reluctant feminisation.

For adult readers aged 18+ only

Introduction

The Submissive Sissy is an updated and edited book based on an earlier book called *Her Toy*.

The Submissive Sissy carries on from *A Very Dominant Woman*. I wrote it after several readers wanted to know what happened next to Sissy Stephanie, one of the two main characters from this book. The other is Aretta Ademola — a very dominant mistress.

The Submissive Sissy begins in Aretta's home. We find Stephanie is now a very Submissive Sissy with a new sissy-bimbo name. Aretta had plans for her sissy. Her plans do not include sissy returning to masculinity. Ever.

Quite the opposite.

Chapter 1

A short skirt

His penis showed from below the hem of his miniskirt. The pink pleated skirt was little more than a three-inch-long frill around his waist.

He stood in the entrance hall by the front door waiting for his Mistress's guest to arrive. Mistress Melissa. He'd met her once before and it hadn't gone well for him.

He glanced at his slim wrist. The delicate small feminine watch had a thin leather strap. It was 6.55 pm. They were due in five minutes. His legs felt like jelly, his penis twitched and his smooth balls hung loose.

Mistress Ademola wanted him this way. And to wait by the door. She didn't like her friends having to wait. The black glossy front door reflected his distorted image. He hardly recognised himself from the person who'd first met Ms Ademola a year ago. Back then he was Steven and he'd had a wife. That had been a lifetime ago.

Since Aretta had taken him to be her live-in sissy maid, she'd reduced the length of his skirts. Today was the shortest he'd ever worn. It was less a skirt than a small frill around his waist. She hadn't allowed him the dignity of panties. His penis and balls hung free and on view below the hem.

His blouse was stretched taut over his giant breast forms. He tugged on the skirt. He wasn't sure why, it was never going to be long enough. He looked at his watch again: 6.56 pm.

She'd been hinting at a change in his circumstances for a few days. She first feminised him at work and then transferred him to work at her home as her housemaid. He'd been Stephanie then but Aretta considered this too normal. She said he needed a name that was more suitable for a sissy bimbo. Candi.

A bead of sweat slid down his temple. His throat was dry. Why was Aretta making him greet her friend in a skirt that exposed him this way? She was up to something. And it would be a step up from what she had subjected him to so far.

She grinned again. "You're wondering why I want your genitals on display for my friend."

He swallowed hard and nodded,

looking to the floor.

"It's the next stage of your training. You see, Candi, you are still not submissive enough."

He looked up at her for a moment, perplexed.

"I see, you do not yet comprehend your situation." She folded her arms across her large breasts. She looked to the ceiling as if searching there for words. She looked back at him. "I want you to be like a willing puppy. And what does a willing puppy do when it wants to show submission to its mistress?"

She was toying with him. "I don't know Mistress Ademola."

Aretta sidled over to him. She put her hand over his penis and balls. Her dark-brown fingers caressed his smooth balls. She then running her long red talons along the length of his penis. It shot to a massive erection.

She took her hand away. "Oh, I say. What happened there, Candi?"

"I'm sorry Mistress," he mumbled.

She put her hand back to his erection. "Not to worry, Candi. I like to see you enjoying being my sissy maid."

She suddenly dug her nails into his balls. He yelped.

"You need to understand I own you and your body. I will do whatever I pleased with you." She thought for a second. "Ah, yes, the puppy, I almost forgot."

She released her grip and he breathed out in deep relief. Her hands flowed around his balls, finding the little balls inside his testes. She clamped her hand around them. He screamed.

She maintained her grip. "When a puppy wants to show submission it lays on its back, opens its legs and displays its genitals. The ultimate sign of submissive vulnerability. Genital display."

Aretta let go and tears watered in his eyes. The dull pain lay in his stomach.

"And that is why I want your genitals displayed this evening." She stroked his face. "Sissy, bimbo and puppy."

Aretta returned to the end of the entrance halls and leaned against the wall. She was waiting for the arrival of Mistress Melissa and his discomfort. She loved to see him in humiliated discomfort.

He passed his fingers through his

long fair hair; it was an involuntary feminine movement these days. He was using more and more feminine movements. They came naturally now.

His bleach blond hair flowed over his shoulders and down to his shoulder blades. The days of short hair had long gone. As had the brown and greying colour.

He ran his fingers through his hair again and a finger caught in the large hoop of one earring. It was 6.58.

He felt hot and clammy at the thought of more ignominy at Aretta's hands once her guest arrived. Yet, it was a scintillating combination of utter horror and deep excitement.

He had another problem. Despite Aretta squeezing his balls, he remained hard. Aretta spotted it and let out a sharp growl of a laugh.

As he waited, his mind drifted back to his previous life. He'd had a normal life with a normal past wife. Rebecca. Sweet Rebecca couldn't handle his descent into femininity and being a sissy. That life was no more; he was now Candi and he belonged to Aretta Ademola, his mistress and owner. She was a very dominant lady.

The doorbell sounded with a dull flat buzz. He moved forward to open the door. His erection stood out firm and strong.

Chapter 2
Humiliation

The door swung back. He threw back his long blonde hair as he stood to the side. The imperious Melissa swept in. Melissa was always punctual.

She was dressed as if ready for a business meeting. She wore a dark skirt, matching jacket and black high-heeled stilettos. A small boyish-looking girl followed behind her. The girl looked frightened. He'd never met her before but he guessed she was Melissa's housemaid, Fifi. He wondered why Melissa had brought her this evening, she'd never bothered before. He shut the door behind them, the door handle squealing as if in pain.

Fifi stared at him with large rabbit-like eyes as if in shock. He curtsied to Melissa. Melissa looked at him with disdain then down to his erection. She sniffed dismissively. That made him harder.

Melissa glared into his eyes for a moment. "Glad to see you're ready."

He froze. What did that mean? Fifi's eyes widened as she looked down at his erection. She tore them away and followed her Mistress into the expansive living room.

He followed them, conscious his erection was swinging as he stumbled on his heels. Aretta saw him. "Get Mistress Melissa a drink, puppy girl."

Melissa sniggered.

He went into the kitchen area and returned with a glass of white wine on a silver tray.

Melissa was sitting on the large square sofa, next to Aretta. He served their drinks and curtsied, his erection waved hard in the cool air of the apartment.

"Her clitty and pussy balls are a little large for a sissy, Aretta," said Melissa. "What will you do to shrink them?"

A shot of fear ran through Candi. He stood up. She had to be teasing him.

"I've been thinking about that. Maybe hormones, maybe a restrictive cage that squashes it flat?" said Aretta.

"A cage would take too long and it won't reduce the balls."

Aretta nodded. "Yes, you're right. I'm open to ideas, Mel."

"Good, I'll send you some details by email. I'd go for hormone therapy."

Candi listened with mounting horror. Hormones did not sound appealing yet the idea somehow made him feel hotter and excited. That was madness.

Fifi was standing in front of the two mistresses. Her head was down, her arms by the side of her black plain housemaid's dress. She looked like a hotel chambermaid except for the thin leather dog collar with small chrome studs.

Melissa held a thin metal chain with a black leather loop handle. It matched

Fifi's collar. He knew something was going on but he didn't know what.

"Candi," said Aretta suddenly. "I usually get you to milk yourself to take all that residual maleness away. Tonight, I have a little treat for you. I want you to get rid of your nasty male juices inside Fifi. Melissa and I will watch. It will be fun."

Candi and Fifi exchanged horrified glances. So this was what was going on and why Melissa had brought Fifi. Fifi's look of horror faded back to expressionless.

Aretta continued, her glacial blue eyes shone like sunlight reflecting from ice. Her unwrinkled ebony face was like chiselled stone.

"Fifi," said Melissa. "I want you to suck Candi's clitty. Don't let her cum yet though."

Candi stood back in shock. Fifi was attractive enough, in a boyish way. In private, he wouldn't have said no. What he didn't want, was to be in a public sex show. Fifi moved towards him, her eyes flat. She complied without debate to her mistress's commands. Like a puppy? Her eyes gave away her displeasure.

"Stay where you are, Candi. Fifi's going to such your clitty and we want to watch," said Aretta.

Fifi was small and slim, almost skinny. She had a boyish figure and short mousey hair. Her mouth moved over his erect penis and warmth engulfed him. Her moist tongue flicked against his raw sensitive penis head.

It had been a long time since anyone had given him a blow job. Aretta and Melissa watched with fascination as Fifi moved her mouth up and down the length of his shaft. Fifi was not his type, he preferred someone more shapely.

Fifi's short bobbed hair and skinny frame were too boyish for him but she was an expert with her mouth.

"Fifi, put some feeling into it," Melissa ordered. "We want you two to be girlfriends."

Girlfriends? This was surreal, not least because He'd never had to perform sex in front of anyone before.

Fifi grabbed his balls and kneaded them like soft dough. It was without the feeling Melissa demanded but she seemed satisfied and sat back to watch. He closed his eyes. He had to try to enjoy things as best he could. The best way was to shut himself away.

"Suck faster, Fifi. Show loving," Aretta ordered. She gigged lightly.

He looked down at Fifi's head was moving back and forth along his erect shaft. Her teeth rubbed against his taut skin. It was exciting and irritating at the same time. Something stirred deep in his balls. He was going to cum if Fifi kept this up.

"Lick the end of her clitty with your tongue, Fifi. It looks like she's about to cum. We want to see it shoot in your face and mouth," Melissa said coldly.

Fifi pulled away. His erection went cool in the air. He closed his eyes again. He was desperate to cum and Fifi had left him hanging in suspense. Fifi's hand closed around the base of his cock. Her tongue lashed shoot against the slit at the end of his penis.

A jolt of electricity surged along his erect shaft. His stomach twisted in anticipation of release. Fifi wiped her tongue around the head of his penis. More electricity shot up his shaft. He groaned, he was losing himself to the sensations swirling around his balls and penis.

Fifi licked against the end of his penis as if it were a lollipop. She was good at this. She stopped a moment as he built up for the moment. He calmed a little, she was playing with him. He forgot about the two mistresses.

She licked again. The stirrings inside his balls grew. His cum stirred and rumbled like a witches cauldron. It shot up his erect shaft and onto Fifi's thin lips and tongue. She cringed away for a moment while maintaining her grip. He groaned in ecstasy as shots of his grey viscous cum spurted onto her cheeks, nose and eyelids. She closed her eyes. Drops slid from her eyelashes.

Fifi let go of his penis and lay back on the floor. She looked away. She wiped his cum from her eye with the back of her hand.

"That was fun," Aretta said, smiling broadly. Her large perfect white teeth glistened in the subdued lighting.

Candi felt awful. How humiliating. His penis hung imply.

"It was," Melissa said. She turned to look at the two maids. "After dinner, we're going to watch you two fuck each other. You are going to be in love so clean yourselves up, prepare our dinner and build up your energy for the next show."

Chapter 3
After-dinner treats

Candi curtsied to the two women sitting on the sofa. He adjusted the little frill of a skirt around his waist.

Fifi got up without expression. She went to the bathroom and he heard the sound of water running as she cleaned her face. She returned and followed him to the kitchen to prepare dinner for their mistresses.

He looked up from the preparation of the food. Fifi averted her eyes to the floor in acute embarrassment. She was cute, he thought. They'd shared an intimacy. Although forced, it was not unpleasant, even in full view of the mistresses.

Here they were, thrown together for the amusement of their owners. Having some help from the plain-looking Fifi made his work easier. She was obviously well trained. Aretta only wanted to humiliate men but he knew Melissa liked anyone weaker than her, male or female.

The two maids worked in silence, there was nothing to say. Candi thought about the time he'd met Melissa's submissive office assistant, Joanne. He had seen Joanne when Melissa had last visited. Melissa also used Joanne as her driver. She had driven Melissa there and waited in the hall for the whole evening.

Joanne had worn a short pink pleated skirt, white blouse, high heels and had long flowing hair. Candi hadn't realised at first that Joanne had once also been a man. Aretta had told him that she would, one day, finish transforming him from a nasty male into a perfect submissive girl. As Melissa had done to Joanne.

The two maids served dinner to their mistresses. They are their food in the kitchen, still in silence. Aretta called them to come to them. They left the kitchen together.

The two mistresses had returned to the sofa and were chatting amicably. Aretta looked up. "Remove your clothing, both of you."

Candi and Fifi exchanged horror-filled glances. They remembered Melissa's warning of what was expected. They exchanged another glance. Together in humiliation. Candi removed his blouse and placed it on the floor. He smoothed down his thick rich blonde hair.

"Stop," it was Aretta. She looked puzzled. Remove each other's clothes.

That would be more fun. Fifi, you first. Take off Candi's clothes."

"That's a good idea Aretta," Melissa agreed nodding slightly in satisfaction. "And kiss while you do it."

"Great idea."

The mistresses were egging each other on with ideas.

Fifi shrugged almost imperceptibly. He thought he spotted a tiny roll of her expressionless eyes. Maybe it was his imagination. Fifi unclipped his bra and looked surprised as two large rubber breast forms fell to the floor. They landed like two wobbling over-large fried eggs onto the floor.

She kissed him lightly. It felt nice and she smelled nice. Fifi then unzipped the back of his skirt and pulled it down over his dark stockings to the floor. He stepped out of it, it made little difference anyway, it was so short.

He balanced unsteadily on his high heels. His penis began to recover from the earlier ejaculation. Fifi looked at his smooth hairless genitals as she removed his shoes and stockings.

Fifi stood and kissed him again.

"Open your mouths, for pity's sake," said Melissa.

He opened it a little and moved his head sideways to kiss properly. She tasted minty. His penis jerked to attention.

Fifi pulled away and waited her turn. He unzipped the back of her chambermaid's dress and let it fall to the floor He unclipped her bra. Two small shapely breasts stood firm. They looked like a young teenager's breasts. She was too boyish for his taste but he didn't get a choice any more.

Fifi had bare legs and a pair of plain

flat practical shoes. She wore a large pair of large black panties. He hesitated and Fifi continued to look blank.

"Take her panties off, Candi," said Aretta.

He knelt and slid her thick cotton panties down in one thrust. A small erect penis stood out in his face. He recoiled and fell back on the floor.

"Suck her little clitty, Candi. It's only fair, She did it to you," Aretta said again.

He looked across not knowing what to do. It was a penis. Fifi was a male. Aretta was holding Melissa's hand, rubbing the back of it with a free thumb. Everything was hitting him at once. Fifi was a male and he'd sucked him off. Aretta was holding hands with Melissa. The word was turning upside down.

Fifi laid back and spread his legs open without enthusiasm. His little penis poked up hard and erect. Fifi was following orders and he guessed she'd done this before.

This was awful. Suck a penis? However, he had no choice. It was what Aretta wanted. it wouldn't do to question her. From his kneeling position, he moved over Fifi and face his erection. He smelled

Fifi's sex.

He moved down and put his mouth over the little erection. It tasted odd, salty. A stronger sexual smell flooded his nostrils. He moved his mouth all the way over Fifi's erection. A slight sensation of disgust hit him. And his own erection hardened.

He looked momentarily towards Aretta and Melissa. Aretta's dark slim muscular arm moved to the back of the sofa and stroked the back of Melissa's head.

He averted his eyes and slipped his

tongue onto Fifi's penis. A stronger taste of salty and something warm and gooey slipped into his mouth. He swallowed and shuddered. Had he just swallowed Fifi's pre-cum?

Despite Fifi's feigned indifference, he was rock hard and leaking pre-cum. He drank it in. Candi's cock stiffened more strongly at the feeling on his tongue. Fifi's flavours were in his mouth and his smell in his nostrils.

Fifi came without warning. Warm cum spurted into his mouth. Fifi made no sound but pulled his head to her crotch and arched his back. Candi swallowed without thinking and shuddered at the taste and the thought of what he'd done. And his penis was rock hard.

He glanced toward Aretta and Melissa. Aretta watched him as her fingers played with Melissa's ear. Melissa stroked Aretta's dark ebony leg just above her knee. She slipped her long red fingernails under the hem and lifted her dress a couple of inches.

"I now want you to enter Fifi from behind," Aretta said dreamily. "And come closer so we can see better."

Candi and Fifi shuffled across in front of the two mistresses. Fifi bent over on all fours. Melissa stood and walked round to the other side of the two sissies on the floor.

Fifi's bottom faced him. He saw his two small balls hanging with the limp penis. Fifi's hole appeared large. This would not be the first time for Fifi.

Chapter 4
The show

Melissa took Candi"s penis with two fingers like it was a piece of dirt. She slapped gel around it. Her face grimaced theatrically as she pull him towards Fifi's waiting bottom. Melissa then rested on her haunches inches away from him.

Aretta leant forward, putting one elbow on her knee and cupping her chin in an elegant hand. "Make love, sissies." She smiled mischievously, her face almost on his erection.

He failed to understand why he was

so erect. This was awful. Wasn't it?

"Come on, put it into your new lover," Melissa ordered.

He moved his penis tip to touch Fifi's waiting hole. He saw it flinch a little.

"Pu it in, sissy," said Aretta

He pushed and it slid in smoothly.

"All the way," said Melissa.

He pushed it deep into Fifi's hole, the walls of her bumhole were tight against the head of his erection. He pushed in slowly, this was not so awful as he'd expected. Fifi gave a low moan. He pushed in until it was all the way. He withdrew a little and plunged his erection into her again. He felt it touch against something and Fifi groaned again.

He had never felt so hard; something about this was exciting. He closed his eyes to try to shut the two Mistresses out. He moved in and out of Fifi, his balls slapping against Fifi's balls as he moved. Fifi began to move his body to the rhythm of his thrusts. He was going to come if this continued. That was also unexpected.

He moved faster as the feelings of orgasm engulfed him. He came hard. Fifi squealed and he open his eyes. She had also cum and had splattered her juices on the floor below. Candi groaned and fell back. His juices oozed from Fifi's bum.

"Excellent show," Aretta said.

Melissa returned to the sofa and sat up close to Aretta again. Melissa moved her hand back to Aretta's leg, a fingertip above her knee.

Aretta pointed a long dark finger at the floor below Fifi. Her talon-like red fingernail was long and sharp like a razor. "Candi, be a good sissy. Lick up Fifi's mess."

Candi looked to Aretta in astonishment, then to Fifi's puddle of cum. Before he had a chance to process her words, Melissa stood, grabbed his ear and pulled him towards the pool of cold cum. She pushed his face in it. "Lick."

The smell of cold cum make him try to recoil; the slime went up his nose. Melissa's hand remained on his ear. She twisted it and a sharp rack of pain shot down his neck. She pulled his face in the cum and he licked and swallowed. He retched but carried on.

Melissa pulled his head up by his ear. "Better."

He wiped some of the goo away from

his nose and around his mouth.

"Time for bed for you two lovebirds," said Aretta. "Fifi, you will sleep with Candi, your new girlfriend. I'm sure you'll want to kiss cuddle and play some more." Aretta looked deeply into Melissa's eyes. "And you can come with me."

The two Mistresses took each other's hands and walked to Aretta's bedroom. Aretta closed the door behind them.

Candi stood from the damp patch on the floor, his limp cock hanging like a piece of string. Fifi's eyes flitted momentarily to it, the first sign of any interest in him.

"It seems you're going to have to share with me," he said.

"Don't worry, Candi," Fifi replied. They smiled at each other.

They tramped to Candi's bedroom and got into bed. They turned away from each other but Candi could not sleep. That evening had been a big moment. Things had escalated beyond anything he'd ever imagined.

"Are you awake, Fifi?" said Candi. The events of the evening played back in his mind like a bad porn movie. He'd had full sex with a male. OK, Fifi was hardly masculine but even so; a line had been crossed.

"Yes, I can't sleep," said Fifi.

He felt Fifi turn and he turned to face him. lA couple of hours earlier they had never met before and now they were naked in bed together having had

"My name is really Stephen," said Candi. "I went to work for Aretta and she turned me into this."

Fifi pushed himself up on his elbows. "No, it's not, you're Candi now. You need to accept this and devote yourself to

Aretta." Fifi showed a firmer side for the first time.

"My point is, it's difficult, Fifi. I don't understand the conflicting feelings I have. I am devoted to Aretta but she treats me badly, humiliates me and makes me do awful things. Yet I love it and her."

"Of course. Aretta has chosen you. She has a strong affection for you, in a submissive slave sort of way. This is why she treats you as she does. She's not treating you badly she's bestowing a wonderful gift on you. It's the gift of being utterly dominated but also cared for."

Candi was not convinced it was a gift but he knew there was no point in debating it. Fifi had been turned and accepted his life.

Fifi continued. "You don't have to think or want for anything. Aretta will choose every aspect of your life for you. Remember, this is a privilege. You are hers and that is a beautiful thing. Every humiliation she heaps on you should be considered a gift and you should thank her. You're going through an adjustment in your approach to life. That's a major event, I understand that. Eventually, given time, you'll understand it too and you'll be at peace."

"I'm not sure."

"You can speak to me at any time, if our mistresses permit it. I can give you advice to help you in your journey. I'll ask Melissa's permission for you to call me. I'm sure they will both agree as it will help you to accept your fate and they will want us to continue having sex."

"OK," Candi said, doubtfully.

"And one last thing," Fifi added as he was pulling the covers up ready to sleep. "Be ready for the next step. Aretta has many more gifts to bestow on you. She'll want your feminisation to go further and deeper. Be prepared. She's going to want you to look and act like a slutty bimbo. I know her well enough to see this. She has already pushed you some way down that track and I can see you've accepted that you are no longer a real man any more. But, the most difficult changes are yet to come. You will have to embrace them and enjoy your new life."

Candi swallowed hard. This was not what he wanted to hear. It was too definite and too permanent.

"And you need to accept me. Our mistresses expect us to be lovers so we will. We have no choice. We have to act as sissy sluts for them." Fifi leant across and kissed Candi gently on the lips. "Let go and accept the gift of becoming a sissy." Fifi took his hand and placed it on one of her small pert breasts.

"Where did they come from?" said Candi.

"Various supplements Mistress Melissa gives me. It's a balance, she says she likes to see me perform with other sissies so she likes my clitty functioning."

With that, Fifi removed Candi's hand and turned over. "Goodnight. Lover."

That didn't help his concerns but it did explain the road Aretta was going to take him. He looked at the ceiling as Fifi's deep breathing became rhythmic.

"What more could Aretta expect from me?" he whispered to himself.

He was about to find out.

Chapter 5
Pegged

Candi came out of the shower rubbing himself with a large pink fluffy towel. He yawned. Last night had been weird. Fifi had already showered and was sitting at the plain dressing table combing his hair.

Fifi wore only the pink leather dog collar as Aretta didn't want them dressed. His small breasts were pert and looked a little out of place on Fifi's thin body with no hips and a flat bottom.

They had shared two intense sexual sessions last night. The atmosphere that morning was unspoken embarrassment, despite their chat in bed. The realisation of the events hung in the morning air without being said. They went about their preparations in the same small room. They nudity was a stark reminder of their situation.

Fifi's words last night did resonate in his mind. He had to accept Arettais gift to him. The gift of being turned into a sissy.

They heard Melissa call out. "Sissies. Breakfast. Now."

They left the bedroom to see Aretta and Melissa sitting opposite each other at the dining room table. They wore matching silk dressing gowns and satisfied expressions.

The sissy maids made coffee for their mistresses and delivered it to them. Candi didn't know why the mistresses wanted them naked. They made breakfast, served it with a curtsey, and returned to the kitchen to have coffee and toast by themselves. They sat in silence on kitchen stools next to each other at the large bar.

Fifi looked at Candi's penis and balls without shame. "You have a cute clitty," he said.

He took Candi's penis in her fingers and looked at his balls. Candi pushed him away. "What are you doing?"

Fifi grabbed it again. "Our mistresses want us to be lovers, this is how it has to be."

Candi went to speak but shut his mouth. Fifi stroked his penis with a thumb. It jerked a little and Fifi smiled.

"Girls," Aretta called.

"What do they want now?" Candi said then realised he had been enjoying the intimacy.

Fifi looked at him sternly. He was too

well-trained to complain about her mistress or anyone else's mistress. Fifi's creased forehead told him to behave.

"The Mistresses come first," Fifi said in a low voice. "We can play some more later." A glint of passion sparked in his eyes

Candi still had to learn to accept instructions without a pang of rebelliousness inside. He hid it well most times. There was wisdom in Fifi's simple words.

They slid off their stool and entered the dining area. They stood together in front of their mistresses. Candi felt a deep discomfort in his nakedness again. The maids curtsied.

"Sissies," said Aretta. "When you're together and naked, I expect you to hold each other's clitties. It's a sign of affection."

Fifi's hand moved across and wrapped around Candi's genitals.

"Candi?"

He quickly put his hand around Fifi's penis.

Aretta nodded. Melissa stood from the table. Her gown was open; a large strap-on cock protruded from it. She walked around to stand behind Candi. He felt her hand on the back of his head. She pushed it to bend him over.

He felt the tip of the strap-on pressed against his bum. There was the chill of cold gel. Surely not. The false penis was at least eight inches long.

It stayed against his hole for several seconds. It wasn't as if he hadn't been pegged before. Aretta's friend. Mistress Anne, his former work colleague had done it when he first moved in to be Aretta's maid.

There was a shot of pain and the dildo entered him. He took a sharp intake of breath. Melissa pushed it in slowly and steadily. It went in to the hilt and he felt the smooth leather of her belt against his bottom cheek.

It filled him up, it was far larger than the one Mistress Anne had used. His eyes watered. Mistress Melissa withdrew it methodically and then plunged it in deep and firm. Her open silk gown flicked against his legs. He gritted his teeth, trying not to squeal. It was more the shock than any pain.

He felt a sharp tingle as the end of

the dildo pressed against something sensitive inside him. His penis sprung to attention, hard and firm.

Melissa withdrew the dildo to its tip. He remained bending, expecting it to be thrust back in. Nothing happened. He heard Melissa move away. It hadn't been as bad as he'd expected but better it had stopped.

"We wanted to teach you a little lesson, Candi," Aretta said. "You need to be regularly entered. It's what sissies need." She let the words sink in. "You are a submissive servant, a sissy but not a real woman. Real women are superior to sissies we have to force-feminise. It's not the same."

"Fifi, now you will enter Candi," said Melissa.

It was still morning and they were having to perform for the mistresses.

He watched through his legs as Fifi approached behind him. Fifi's small hairless penis pointed at his bottom like a bullet. He tensed as Fifi got closer. He felt the tip of his penis against his hole. It entered him tentatively. It was far smaller than Melissa's dildo. Fifi slid his erection fully into his hole.

Although smaller, Fifi's penis tip pressed against that spot inside him as before. He liked the feeling. He'd never experienced this when he was with his wife. He would cum quickly if Fifi kept pressing his penis against that spot.

Fifi moved his hips in a circular movement. It was incredible. He'd never felt this before and Fifi had clearly done this before. Candi thought his penis would burst it was so hard with the intensity of the sensations he was feeling.

Suddenly his dam burst and he came with a spurt onto the hardwood floor below him. Fifi continued to thrust then froze and jerked. The inside of his hole went warm and gooey. Fifi pulled out and Candi felt a drop of warm cum oozing from his behind.

Aretta stood. "Clean up your mess, sissies"

He started to stand.

"No," she said. "You'll clean it as before by licking it up and swallowing it." She turned to Fifi. "While Candi is bending over licking up her mess, you'll lick your mess from her pussy hole."

Candi looked up at her in shock. What more demeaning things would she think up? He stayed still for a moment considering the alternative of saying no. He didn't want to lick up his sperm and he did not want Fifi licking his behind. He remembered what Fifi had said to him.

He looked behind at Fifi. He raised his eyebrows as a reminder to do as Aretta said. Candi got on his knees and bent to lick up his cum. It was cold and salty and mixed with dust. A warm feeling went against his bottom. Fifi's tongue lashed into his hole and slurped.

Aretta and Melissa laughed. This was utter humiliation.

Chapter 6
Make-over

Aretta offered to take Melissa and Fifi home by car after breakfast. And after our floor show.

This meant Candi would be the driver. Aretta had told him a week ago that his new role was also to be her driver and it was now time. There was a large car park in the basement beneath the apartment block.

Aretta and Melissa had gone through Candi's clothing like two giggling schoolgirls. They wanted to dress him in bimbo clothes. They chose a short white ra-ra skirt in white chiffon.

Candi held it up. A more feminine item of clothing he couldn't imagine. A bolt of electricity shot through his belly at the excitement of wearing the soft frilly skirt. His penis was spent after the session with Fifi but it jerked at the thought of putting this skirt on and going out.

Aretta pulled out a dining room chair. "Sit there, Candi, once you've put your pretty sissy skirt and blouse on. And don't forget the bra and breast inserts."

He dressed and guessed he was to star again in another of Aretta's games.

Aretta and Melissa were power dressed in business suits with knee-length skirts. They sat together on the sofa waiting. Fifi walked towards him with brushes, a large black hairdryer and a leather bag.

"Fifi is a trained beautician," Melissa explained.

So that was their plan.

"Before we go out, I want you to look pretty and girly," Aretta said coolly. "You're to be my sissy bimbo. You'll never wear anything but sissy clothing again. And you will never have sex with a real woman ever again: sissies and men only." She leaned forward. "Because you are a girl now." She tapped his nose and sat back.

He felt a pang at her words. This was real and she was clear. He was to remain a sissy forever, there was no going back to manhood. No going back to his wife.

Fifi set to work. He put Candi's hair in curling tongs. He waited until it curled and undid the tongs and sprayed hairspray in. Once he'd finished curling, he worked on Candi's long fingernails. Fifi cleaned off the ivory nail polish with remover; the acrid chemical smell of the liquid burned into his nostrils.

Once cleaned, Fifi painted each of his fingernails in bright luminous pink.

"You have lovely long nails, Candi," said Fifi.

"Thank you," he mumbled looking at his half-inch-long fingernails covered in pink polish.

Fifi kneeled and painted his toenails with the same colour. He then applied makeup including bright pink lipstick.

Fifi stood back and looked at Candi.

"Finished."

Aretta and Melissa giggled again. He was surprised at their occasional change from elegant, sophisticated dominant ladies to giggling schoolgirls. They were enjoying making him look like an exaggerated sissy bimbo. Maybe this was what Fifi had meant last night by saying that there was further to go in his feminisation.

Fifi tied a pink ribbon to the back of his waving curling blond hair. into a large bow. He felt top-heavy, his breast inserts were much larger. Thankfully they weren't real, he thought.

Candi stood up. He shuffled his hips. He felt his balls falling out of the tiny panties.

"Stop fiddling, sissy," said Aretta.

"My balls are falling out. My panties are too small," said Candi.

"Of course they are." Aretta stood and put the back of her hands on her hips. She pointed to a pair of silver open-toed sandals.

"You will wear these today," Aretta said.

He slid his feet into the sandals. The thin-strapped shoes were higher then anything he'd worn before. He guessed the thin shiny heels to be five inches. How would he manage? He had no choice. He would also be tall in these. He'd stand out more, taller than Aretta or Melissa. He must be around six-foot-three. There was no hiding place.

"No stockings today, I like seeing lots of leg flesh on show. Especially with those shoes." Aretta chuckled into her hand.

"I look like a bimbo," he complained.

"Exactly. That is how I want you to look," said Aretta. "There is still some work to do but I will get you there."

The two friends did their schoolgirl giggle again. They seemed to be enjoying making him look like this. He stared at himself, a cartoon image of a distant schoolboy fantasy. What did she mean by a bit of work to do yet? Fifi had warned him but he'd imagined it was bigger hair, shorter skirts if that were possible. And pinker.

He looked down and his long exposed legs. Hold on. He lifted his lightweight skirt. It was see-through.

He looked up to see Aretta with a wide smirk. "The material is so thin, it's see-through."

"I know. Is that not wonderful?" Aretta said. "Everyone will see your bottom. Exposure, remember? Now stop fussing it is time to leave."

He felt nervous anticipation. Melissa had the dog lead in her hand and the chain was attached to Fifi's neck. Fifi accepted this without complaint or expression. It was how it was.

The four of them left Aretta's flat and walked to the lift at the end of the corridor. It was a strange group. The tall strong Aretta and Melissa were well-groomed in high-quality business wear. Fifi wore in a maid's dress and on a lead.

And Candi, the tallest of the group, had masses of long bleach blond hair, a tiny skirt with long bare legs, huge breast forms and vertiginous heels.

They took the lift to the car park below the apartment block. They went to the basement and made their way to Aretta's long black Mercedes. After holding the doors open for the mistresses to get in the back and curtseying, Candi got in. He drove out of the underground car park, waited for the automatic gates to open, and up into the street.

Melissa's townhouse was in a gated community in the up-and-coming eastern side of the city. Candi stopped outside the gates and Melissa and Fifi got out.

Candi turned to face Melissa in the back. "Home, Mistress?"

Aretta's face broke into a wide toothy grin. "No. We have an appointment to discuss the next phase of your development."

That was the first he had heard of that. "What next phase, Mistress?"

Aretta's grin became wider. "You will find out when we get there. Head for the city centre, there's a good sissy."

Chapter 7
The appointment

Candi's mind was working overtime with mounting panic. He drove through the slow city traffic back towards the city centre. After thirty minutes, Aretta gave him an address and told him to find a car park there. It was on the other side of the city centre. Candi punched the postcode into the car's navigation.

They arrived and Candi took the car into a public underground car park behind a busy high street.

They got out and took the stairs to

the street level. They left through a stiff door and stepped into a green square. The large trees were in blossom, the grass perfect. Signs were dotted around the park warning people to keep off the grass and no balls games.

This was an exclusive area, the residents did not appreciate noise or disruption. The street was full of people carrying shopping bags with expensive brand names on them.

Aretta walked ahead. "Say three paces behind me." She strode along the pavement with similar Georgian buildings on either side.

Candi tottered behind Aretta, struggling to keep up in his unfamiliar five-inch heels. His eight, exposed legs, tiny skirt and piles of blond hair attracted attention from other pedestrians in the midday sun. It was an unusually warm spring day.

He fought the light breeze. It threatened to lift the light chiffon to expose a bum covered only by a submerged g-string. Several people spotted his skirt was all but transparent in the spring sunshine.

Aretta turned to a building. She buzzed on a button by an enormous black wooden door. It opened and Aretta pushed through and strode to a desk. An attractive young lady looked up. She was like a younger version of Aretta.

"Appointment for Candi. 12.30. Laser hair removal,"

He stepped back. A cold chill went down his spine. Laser hair removal. That sounded permanent.

The receptionist looked at her screen. "Jessica's waiting. Go straight through to room four."

Aretta took him by the hand and pulled him to the room. She entered after knocking, not waiting for a reply. A slim thirty-something lady stood up from behind a desk. She greeted them with a cool smile and looked up at Candi. "Sit here." She pointed to a chair by the desk.

He sat and pulled on his tiny skirt. Aretta paced behind him, she was impatient about something.

Jessica's smile dropped for a split second before regaining her composure. It was obvious he was not a real woman.

Jessica sat behind her desk and turned to the side to speak to Candi. She crossed her legs and fidgeted with her white medical coat. "Ms Ademola says you've asked to have your body hair permanently removed." She crossed her eyebrows and looked at her written notes. "And you want your pubic hair permanently designed into a feminine triangle shape?"

He choked.

"Yes she does," Aretta answered impatiently. "She wants to be a girl. I am paying so please get on with things, Jessica."

"This is no problem, Ms Ademola, but I need to hear Carla tell me she agrees to the treatment. For legal reasons. And she'll need to sign the papers."

"Yes, of course," Aretta replied. "Candi, tell Jessica how you want your hair permanently removed and you want to be a girl."

Candi choked again. He hadn't expected permanent hair removal. He thought about what Fifi had told him. Aretta was determined he become a sissy girl so it was possibly a natural step.

His eyes swivelled from Jessica to Aretta. "Er, er, I don't know," he stammered.

Jessica looked at Aretta, confused. Aretta marched to Candi and leaned over him. "Tell her."

He turned to Jessica. "Er, yes. I do." He may as well get on with it rather than put up some resistance and lose the fight anyway. In the end, Aretta's money would ensure the clinic did the work. They were just looking for an excuse.

Aretta looked at him. "And tell Jessica how you want her to shape your pubic hair in a feminine triangle."

He swallowed hard. "Please shape my pubic hair into a feminine triangle."

"Excellent," said Jessica, her eyebrows still knitted.

She pointed to the medical bed in the corner. "Remove your clothing and lay on the couch so we can start."

Candi sat back. "Excuse me?"

"I've reserved the whole afternoon for the work. I'll start with your genitals," she said unsteadily.

"Now?" said Candi.

Chapter 8
Denuded

"Hurry up, sissy," an impatient Aretta said. "I've got things to do. You can keep your shoes on. Remove the remainder of your clothes as the nice lady asked."

He was barely decent anyway. He removed his clothing. Jessica sat back at her desk and pretended to type on her laptop but glanced over the screen at times. Once naked, he shivered and wrapped his arms around himself.

He walked to the bed wearing only high-heeled shoes, conscious more than ever due to his height in the heels.

He lay down on a tall medical bed. Jessica got up and walked to him with an artificial nonchalance. She slapped on white latex gloves and grabbed his penis. She twisted it aside and inspected his balls and scrotum area.

"Don't worry, Candi, I get lots of transgenders," she smiled. "This is normal."

"Transgender? I'm not a transgender. It's that Aretta likes me to look this way." He considered himself a man who Aretta had forced to dress as a female."

"Don't think of her as a transgender, Jessica, think of her as a sissy," Aretta said sternly. "It's not the same thing."

Jessica looked up, still holding his penis. "And the difference?"

Aretta grinned. "A sissy is a man who likes to wear extremely feminine clothes and use feminine styles. Like Candi."

He didn't consider he liked to look like this. Aretta forced him. Didn't she? At that moment, his penis started to get harder. Jessica let go and stepped back.

"Sorry," he said, turning bright red.

"I forgot to milk her before we got

here. Have you got a bowl, I'll do it now so you don't have to deal with a nasty erection?" Aretta got up and tutted as she shook her head.

Jessica passed a small chrome bowl to Aretta. Aretta gave it to Candi. "Sit up, milk yourself into the bowl, clean up and lie back again so Jessica can get on with her work," she said.

Jessica stood away. It's not necessary Ms Ademola, I'm not sure this is helpful."

"Don't worry, Jessica, just look away. It won't be pleasant I know but I need to clean out her male urges." She shook her head again. "This is a big problem with sissies. It is a shame there is no pill sissies can take to dry out their nasty mess."

Candi took the bowl meekly with eyes that said he did not want to do this.

"Get on with it, sissy" Aretta demanded loudly.

In the event, Jessica couldn't tear her eyes away from the scene unfolding before her. Candi had to comply. He began to rub his penis with reluctance. He held it over the bowl. Jessica's eyes became wider. He exploded into the blow and light ting from the first jet of sperm hit the bottom of the bowl. He squeezed out the last drops Jessica passed him a wet-wipe while staying back as far as possible.

"Are you ready now?" she asked meekly.

"Yes," he choked, putting the tissue to one side.

Aretta sat down on the other side of the room. Jessica pulled over a large machine from the corner. She switched it on and pulled out a gun-type device.

"Are you sure, Candi? This machine destroys the hair follicles. Your body hair will never regrow."

He looked over to Aretta. "She's sure," said Aretta.

Jessica began to zap the hair roots around his penis and balls. Aretta picked up her phone. It was going to be a long afternoon.

Sometime later, Jessica switched off the laser machine. "Finished."

Candi rubbed his chin. Nothing, not a whisker, it was as smooth as a baby's skin. Even after shaving with the best wet shave razors, he had always felt some residual stubble. Now there was nothing, just smooth skin.

He looked down at his genitals. A tuft of triangular-shaped pubic hair was the only hair below his neck.

Aretta stood and walked to him. "Excellent. You are getting where I want you. You have one more process to get closer."

He shuddered, what more could he go through? He dressed and they left the clinic. A cool evening breeze swept up the street and chilled his bare legs. He walked a couple of paces behind Aretta. She hadn't yet explained what the next process would be.

Chapter 9
An appointment with femininity

The next morning, they were back in the same neighbourhood. They parked in the same car park under the green area.

Candi followed Aretta up the same street, passing the hair removal clinic from yesterday. Candi wore the same high shoes as yesterday but today, Aretta had put him in a little tartan pleated skirt no more than 6 inches long. Aretta had allowed him to wear stockings but they were thin and white with pink bows at the top and front. The tops showed and Candi attracted stares from everyone.

Aretta turned into a similar tall Georgian building and through a large painted door, similar to the one at the hair-removal clinic. Another pretty receptionist looked up and smiled.

"Doctor Martínez, 10.30 appointment," said Aretta.

A doctor, thought Candi. He wasn't ill. What was Aretta up to this time?

"Go straight through to Dr Martínez's office, Ms Ademola," said the receptionist.

Aretta strode to a white panelled door and knocked. They heard a, "Come," from behind the door.

Aretta opened the door and walked in. Candi tottered in behind. Dr. Martínez and Aretta greeted each other like old friends, kissing on both cheeks. Dr. Martínez eyed Candi warily.

Dr Martínez was a lady who appeared to be in her mid-forties with large brown eyes and thick brown hair. He hadn't spotted an accent but she was clearly Spanish or Latin.

"Hello," she smiled pleasantly before her eyes dropped onto his skirt and her face fell hard. "Bimbo."

She was different to the hair removal girl. Dr Martínez was clearly one of Aretta's friends.

"You've done well with this one, Aretta, but I can see her artificial breast forms aren't fully conducive to the look you want to achieve."

Bimbo? Candi was not pleased with the doctor's tone. Aretta looked pleased.

"Remove your top, Candi. Let's see what I have to work with." It was an order from Dr Martínez, not a request. She leaned in to look.

Candi unbuttoned his blouse and

removed his breast forms and then unclipped his bra.

"What's this about, mistress?" he asked looking at Aretta.

The two ladies ignored him. Dr. Martínez put her hands to his chest, feeling around his nipples and pressing his chest muscles. She took a large black felt-tip pen and drew two arc shapes under each chest muscle. Candi couldn't imagine why she was drawing on his chest.

"She's tall, Aretta," Dr Martínez said leaning back and observing Candi's chest above glasses perched on the end of her nose. "She can therefore take large breasts, so the size is up to you. She could carry off a 38C, maybe even a 40C?"

Candi fidgeted in his chair. "You're talking about bust sizes?"

"Yes sissy, of course," said Dr Martínez.

"I want her with enormous breasts. I'm looking for her to be as bimbo as possible," Aretta replied also staring at his chest.

"Breasts?" he said.

Dr Martínez looked at him as if he were odd. Her eyebrows knitted. "Well of course, Candi. If you're to be a proper sissy, you'll need real breasts. Silly girl." She shook her head.

"I don't need tits. I can wear breast forms," he said with increasing alarm.

"Of course you need real breasts, Candi, don't be ridiculous." Aretta huffed in annoyance.

The doctor looked at Aretta. "I think the largest size we could realistically use would be 44C. They would be enormous but they would work."

Aretta nodded, satisfied. "Yes. 44C."

Candi looked back and forth with

horror. Real tits? 44C? *This wasn't happening, was it?*

Dr. Martínez slid a form over to him. "Sign here, Candi. It's a consent-to-operate form and I've just completed the section that says you want to have 44C breasts. And use your legal name. not your sissy name. Stephen Hayley, I believe." She pursed her lips. "For now."

"Yes, I'm Stephen Hayley. But I don't want 44C tits," he said.

"Of course you do, sissy." Dr Martínez looked away, the conversation finished. She scribbled something on a piece of paper. "The gentleman friends Aretta brings you will love your big tits, It's for the best."

"What gentleman friends?" said Candi.

Aretta stood behind him. "Sign the form, sissy." An air of annoyance entered her voice. She didn't like to be contradicted. He remembered Fifi's words.

The two ladies stared at him. Dr Martínez folded her arms. "Now would be nice."

He scribbled a signature.

Dr Martínez grabbed the signed

paper. "I have a slot next week same time, Aretta." Dr Martinez said.

"You're going to be such a bimbo with your enormous breasts, Candi," Aretta said and smiled kindly at him.

He gulped, this wasn't what he wanted but he'd just signed the papers; under pressure. His mind raced. There was always a cooling-off period. He could still say he had changed his mind. He'd signed under duress. Yes, that's what he'd do and he'd speak to Fifi. He said he'd be happy to provide him with advice. And Aretta would be happy they were talking.

Yes, he'd wriggle out of this. 44C tits? Never.

Chapter 10
Mistress rules

The next day he asked Aretta if he could speak to Fifi. She was happy.

He phoned Fifi from his room using Aretta's personal phone. She had one for business.

Fifi answered after several rings. After introductions, Candi explained that Aretta wanted him with real tits and super large.

The line went quiet for a while.

"Candi, what did I tell you?"

"Yes, I know, but this is different.

Aretta wants me with 44C breasts. It's not normal."

He heard Fifi sigh down the phone. "You are one of the luckiest people in the world, Candi."

"How can that be?" Fifi was not making sense to him.

"Listen," Fifi said with patience. "Most men would do anything to be in your position. To be turned into a sissy by a woman like Aretta and to have no worries and no responsibilities. You'll get to wear the sexiest prettiest female clothing. Aretta will pay for anything. She is giving you the gift of real breasts. Stop whinging and go with everything she says."

Candi felt weak. "But it's permanent."

"Exactly. This is her gift to you. Embrace it. Why the hell are you hesitating?"

"It's a big step, Fifi."

"And so is leaving school to go to work. This is just a stage in your development as a person."

"I was born a man. I wasn't meant to be a girl."

"And you won't be a girl. You'll be a bimbo sissy. Forget about the past, embrace your future."

"OK, he said unconvinced. He had to get on with the housework. "I need to go, Fifi, thanks for your advice. I think."

"No problem. And I'll see you tomorrow anyway. Aretta's coming to see Melissa and bringing you. Melissa wants to see us making love again. She said she wants me to cum all over your face and in your mouth."

Fifi had accepted this lifestyle, maybe he had a point. The idea was not without its attractions, he was surprised to think.

He closed the call. Fifi was certain he should have the operation. Was Fifi right though?

Chapter 11
Bimbo

Candi let himself into the apartment. Things had eased lately with Aretta and she gave him more freedom. As long as he cleaned the home and was there to serve her in the evenings, he could do as he pleased.

He closed the door and looked at herself in the large mirror in the hall. It had been a long session at the hairdresser's but it had been worth it. Aretta wanted him with a lighter blond colour and a wave in his long hair. It was to his back. He stroked through his hair with his one-inch long pink nails. His hair fell over his large breasts.

He walked into the living area. Aretta was typing on a laptop. Life was busy for the successful Aretta, one of the world's most successful businesswomen. She needed and deserved Candi's support and devotion. He knew that now. Fifi had explained it to her but it had taken a while to sink in.

Aretta looked up and smiled with satisfaction. Candi curtsied. His white pleated skirt barely extended below her g-string. He lost a little balance on the five-inch high heels but recovered. It would take a little more time to get used to them.

He stood again, it was as if he were standing on tiptoes in these high heels. His tight pink top was cut low across his tits. They had healed nicely. A frilly-edged low-cut 44C bra showed on each side of the massive straining breasts. He had a cleavage you could lose a hand in, Fifi had joked.

Aretta had got his waist down to 28 inches. His top finished just below his tits and the jewellery in his belly button showed.

"Can I get you anything, Mistress?"

"No, sissy. You may relax in your room until my guest arrives."

"Candi curtsied again and said, "Thank you, Mistress." He took small feminine steps back to his room.

The bedroom had no door and neither did his bathroom. Privacy wasn't permitted but that was correct. He didn't deserve privacy, that was something reserved for superior females such as Aretta.

He kicked off his high heels with a relieved sigh and fell onto the bed. His

44C chest bounced inside the straining bra. The small skirt lay across the tiny pleated skirt.

Tonight was to be a new experience. Aretta's guest was her new boyfriend. Aretta had explained Candi was to pleasure her boyfriend. He had had sex with Fifi but Fifi was more like a girl. Candi had met Aretta's new boyfriend once before. He was 6ft 2ins and around 200 pounds of muscle.

And Aretta had explained exactly what pleasure him meant. A blow job. Candi was nervous, this was a big step.

But what Aretta wants, Aretta gets. Without debate.

THE END

I do hope you enjoyed my story. I love the idea of men being made to look like bimbos. If you enjoyed the story please leave me a review write to me at **lady alexa@mail.com.**

Don't forget to read my blog and subscribe to my Forced feminisation and FLR newsletter at

www.ladyalexauk.com

Alexa Martinez (Lady Alexa)

xxx

My other erotic forced feminisation and femdom novels

A Very Dominant Woman

Becoming Joanne 1

Becoming Joanne 2

Becoming Joanne 3

The Reluctant Housemaid

The New Assistant

A Sister-In-Law's Law

Feminisation is Compulsory

How I Feminised my Husband

I am Alexa Martinez, an author and a blog writer from London England. I write on female domination, feminisation, gender transformation and humiliation under my pen name of Lady Alexa.

Subscribe to my blog at www.ladyalexauk.com and subscribe to y newsletter from the blog side panel

Printed in Great Britain
by Amazon